This Little Tiger book belongs to:

Jenifer

15 Farana Drice Lovord

Phone 203624

blesse you sanfor xx

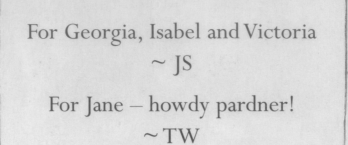

For Georgia, Isabel and Victoria
~ JS

For Jane – howdy pardner!
~ TW

LITTLE TIGER PRESS
An imprint of Magi Publications
1 The Coda Centre, 189 Munster Road, London SW6 6AW
www.littletigerpress.com

First published in Great Britain 2004
This edition published 2005

Text copyright © Julie Sykes 2004
Illustrations copyright © Tim Warnes 2004
Julie Sykes and Tim Warnes have asserted their rights
to be identified as the author and illustrator of this work
under the Copyright, Designs and Patents Act, 1988
All rights reserved

ISBN 1 84506 005 9

A CIP catalogue record for this book
is available from the British Library

Printed in Belgium by Proost NV
2 4 6 8 10 9 7 5 3

Bless You, Santa!

Julie Sykes

Tim Warnes

LITTLE TIGER PRESS

London

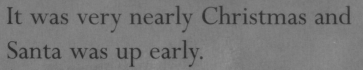It was very nearly Christmas and
Santa was up early.

"Jingle bells, jingle bells," he sang
cheerfully. "Breakfast first and then to work."

He filled the kettle and put on toast, but
as he poured cereal into his bowl Santa's nose
began to tickle.

"*Aah, aah, AAH . . .*

"Atishoo!"

he roared. His sneeze blew
cereal all over the place.

"Bless you, Santa," said Santa's cat, shaking cornflakes out of her tail. "That's a nasty cold."

"Dear me, no!" said Santa in alarm. "It can't be! It's nearly Christmas. I haven't got time for a cold!"

After breakfast Santa rushed to his workshop
and set to work on the unfinished toys. Merrily
he sang as he painted a robot. But Santa's sneezes
were growing larger and louder.
  "Aah, aah, AAH…

"Atishoo!"

"Bless you, Santa," squeaked Santa's little mouse, gathering the beads his sneezes had scattered.

"Bless you, Santa," said Santa's cat, chasing paper stars
as they fluttered around. "You sound awful. Go and
sit by the fire."

"I feel awful!" snuffled Santa. "But I can't rest yet. It's
nearly Christmas and I have to finish these toys or there
will be no presents for all the . . . *Aah, aah, AAH . . .*

"Atishoo!"

Santa sneezed so hard that he slipped over and landed in a stack of balls. Down the balls tumbled, bouncing off Santa and bopping around the room. They crashed into cars, they pushed over paint pots, they toppled the teddies and *ruined* the rockets.

"Atishoo!

"Just look at this terrible mess!"
wailed Santa. "I'll never be ready
in time for Christmas now!"

"Go to bed, Santa," ordered Santa's little mouse. "You're not well. Your nose is so red the reindeer could use it to guide your sleigh! We'll clear up this mess and get everything ready for Christmas."

So Santa's mouse put Santa
back to bed with a mug of hot milk
and a little something to help the cold.
Santa huddled under his duvet.
He sneezed . . .

"Atishoo!"

He snuffled . . .

And finally he snored.

Meanwhile, back in the workshop,
Santa's friends worked as hard as they
could. They mopped . . .

They mended . . .

They glued . . .

They snipped, they stuck and they wrapped.
Faster and faster they toiled until every
single present was finished. Then sleepily
they stumbled off to bed.

Next evening, as the sun set, the animals waited with a sleigh piled high with toys.

"But where is Santa?" asked Santa's cat. "I hope he's better!"

"Who's going to drive the sleigh and deliver all the presents?" asked the reindeer.

"Listen," said Santa's cat. "Can you hear something?" The animals listened.

"It's Santa!" squealed Santa's little mouse. "Are you better, Santa? Can you deliver the presents?"

Santa wrinkled his nose. "*Aah, aah, AAH . . .*

"Ha ha haaa!" chuckled Santa loudly.

"Only joking! I feel much better. Bless you, everyone. You did a great job! Thanks to you all I will get these presents delivered in time for Christmas day."

Santa climbed aboard his sleigh. "Reindeer, up, up and AWAY!" he shouted.

It was a busy night as Santa flew
around the world delivering presents.

When at last Santa landed back at the North Pole
the sun was rising. But he hadn't finished yet.
"These presents are for you," said Santa.
"Presents for us!" squeaked Santa's cat.
"Th . . . Th . . . THAA . . .

"Atishoo!"

Santa's cat sneezed so hard that a pile of snow fell off the trees and buried everyone. "Bless you!" laughed Santa. "And a Happy Christmas to you too!"

Perfect presents from Little Tiger Press

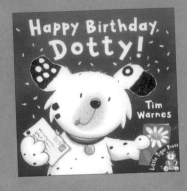

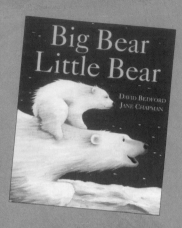

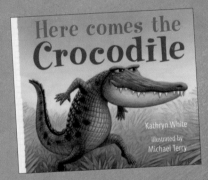

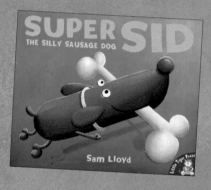

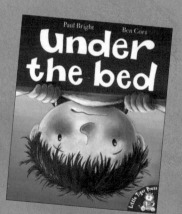

For information regarding any of the above titles
or for our catalogue, please contact us:

Little Tiger Press, 1 The Coda Centre, 189 Munster Road, London SW6 6AW

Tel: 020 7385 6333 Fax: 020 7385 7333

Email: info@littletiger.co.uk

www.littletigerpress.com